ith a pirate, live in a spaceship ith a
ter, wear a suit of armor with sneakers
be a deep-sea diver, build a snowman
you go to the moon, be friends with a
in it, travel by paddle boat, eat sausages
a and wedges, keep a pet monkey, be a
p in a shoe? Or would you go to
n a fairy palace with a ping-pong table
olates, wear a grass skirt with a cowboy
be a hairdresser, go on a bouncy castle
a desert, be friends with a knight, live in
el by helicopter, eat a hamburger, wear
keep a pet spider, be a magician, go
uld you go to the top of a mountain,
house with chandeliers in it, travel by
with rain boots and a sombrero, keep
jigsaw and sleep in a hammock?

In memory of Henry Brown
N. S.

To everyone at Browsers Bookshop
P. G.

First American Edition 2012
Hardcover Edition 2014
Kane Miller, A Division of EDC Publishing

First published in Great Britain in 2003
This edition published by permission of
Random House Children's Books, London
Text © Pippa Goodhart, 2003
Illustrations © Nick Sharratt, 2003

For information contact:
Kane Miller, A Division of EDC Publishing
PO Box 470663
Tulsa, OK 74147-0663
www.kanemiller.com
www.edcpub.com
www.usbornebooksandmore.com

Library of Congress Control Number: 2011931493

Printed and bound in China
10
ISBN: 978-1-61067-342-6

YOU CHOOSE

Imagine you could have anything you wanted!

What sort of things do you mean?

Just turn the pages of this book, have a look and choose.

Words by Pippa Goodhart, pictures by Nick Sharratt

Kane Miller
A DIVISION OF EDC PUBLISHING

If you could go anywhere,

family and friends?

What kind of home

would you choose?

Would you travel with wheels or wings?

Or perhaps choose one of these other things?

When you got hungry,

what would you eat?

Choose some shoes ...

...and perhaps a hat?

Why not get yourself a pet...

Is there a job

you'd like to do?

What would you do...

...for fun?

And when you got tired and felt like a snooze,

where would you sleep? You choose. Good night!

Or would you go to the desert, be fri
with a drum set in it, travel by airship, ea
flops and a furry hat, keep a pet
for fun and sleep in a cradle? Or would
live in a cave with a swimming pool in
wear a tuxedo with Roman sandals and a
on a roller coaster and sleep in a
outer space, be friends with a baby,
on it, travel by steam train, eat a waterm
lacy boots, keep a pet polar bear
and sleep in a hammock? Or would you
live in a cottage with a secret door in it
wear a kilt with clogs and a top
bird-watching and sleep in a nest? Or
be friends with a vampire, live in a tree
space shuttle, eat squid, wear a bow tie
a pet bat, be a deep-sea diver, re